PREHISTORIC TERRITORIES

EPISODE ONE: THE SOUTHERN T-REX

KYLE LEONARD

Outskirts Press, Inc.
http://www.outskirtspress.com

ISBN: 978-1-4787-5172-4

Cover Photo © 2019 Kyle Leonard. All rights reserved - used with permission.

Outskirts Press and the "OP" logo are trademarks belonging to Outskirts Press, Inc.

PRINTED IN THE UNITED STATES OF AMERICA

Dear Reader,

Like you, I grew up loving prehistoric animals and reading about them. I loved watching dinosaurs in the movies, seeing the power of the T. rex and the intelligent hunting of the Velociraptor. I used to imagine what the battles between the dinosaurs were like and how the predators hunted.

As I got older and read new books, along with speaking to paleontologists, my eyes were opened to a whole new view of dinosaur lives. New discoveries found every year showed the dinosaurs with behaviors no one could ever imagine. Thanks to these new discoveries, paleontologists are now getting a better understanding of these animals that once roamed our world.

Now I'm ready to share my knowledge with you and show you a whole new world of dinosaurs and prehistoric animals. Be prepared to view the past in an entirely different way and see what new discoveries are now showing us.

I would like to dedicate this book to my amazing family and my loving girlfriend, Annik, who supported me every step of the way. They inspired me to share my knowledge and educate them about the world of dinosaurs.

Also, a big thank you to my illustrator, Moses, for his excellent and detailed drawings of the animals.

Introduction

Is it possible to rescue prehistoric animals? If so, how would they do in our time? And would they be able to survive in captivity?

My name is Dino Doug, and in this book, you will learn how prehistoric animals lived. You'll see how these animals survived, adapted, and took care of their young. You'll understand what types of environments they lived in, what hazards they faced, and how they defended themselves from their enemies. And see what these amazing creatures were really like in life.

I wrote this book so people could see that prehistoric animals weren't vicious killing machines; instead they were like modern animals, trying to survive and raise their young. And I'll introduce some of the most awesome and bizarre animals that ever lived.

In each chapter, you will learn about animals that you never knew existed. You will learn facts about them and how they lived in their own environments.

Now on to Chapter One. Enjoy your journey through time and remember, extinction will never be forever. Ladies, gentlemen, and children of all ages, welcome to a real wildlife sanctuary.

WELCOME TO PREHISTORIC TERRITORIES.

Chapter One

My dream is coming true. I'm bringing a dinosaur into the twenty-first century.

My entire life I've dreamed of traveling back in time to see real dinosaurs. I always wanted to see what these amazing creatures that once roamed our planet were really like. I wanted to see if they were the true killing machines they're often described as or if they were simple animals trying to survive. I also wanted to see how they took care of their young and what their natural habitats were like.

Years ago, I bought a large territory to build a refuge for prehistoric animals. Most of it was covered in tall trees covering barren ground with small shrubs. There were also large open marshy areas with tall grass and lakes. These are just some of the environments paleontologists believe dinosaurs and other prehistoric animals lived in.

Now it's time to travel back in time to see the dinosaurs and turn the refuge into a park so I can share my dream with other people who have wanted to see prehistoric animals.

As the early morning sun rose over the horizon, I was in my office working on a list. The list included the animals I would be traveling back in time to rescue for the park. It consisted of not just dinosaurs, but animals before and after them.

Down in the park my park keepers and their teams were putting the last touches on the enclosures. The enclosures were designed to house not only dinosaurs, but also animals that lived before and after them.

While I was working on the list, I heard my cell phone go off. I looked at the screen to see it was my friend Dr. Hank Driscoll, a physicist at the Einstein Technological Institute.

"Hey, Hank, how are you, my friend?"

"I'm doing well. I've got good news for you. I have it ready!" Hank said.

"I'm on my way!"

I rushed out of my office as I called my game warden, Ulysses Smith, and told him to meet me at the airstrip near my office right away.

Ulysses was second in charge of my park. He'd spent many years in charge of other parks, mainly in Africa and Asia. His work included protecting endangered animal species.

"Hello, Ulysses. Hank just called me and told me he has it ready," I said.

"You're kidding; what are we waiting for? Let's go!" Ulysses said excitedly.

We got into my plane and headed over to the Institute.

While we flew through the air, Ulysses asked, "Are you excited Hank has it ready for us, Doug?"

"Oh, yeah, I've been waiting for this day my whole life. I've dreamed of traveling back in time to see a real dinosaur. How about you—are you excited?" I asked.

"You bet! I can't wait to see what it looks like and how it works."

We flew to a small airport in New Jersey where a car was waiting to take us to the Institute.

When we got to the Institute, Ulysses and I walked down the hallway toward Dr. Driscoll's lab, getting more excited with each step.

We walked into the lab, where we saw Dr. Driscoll and almost ran up to him.

"Hello, Hank, we're so excited to see what you have for us," I said.

"I'm so glad you're here. This is the most advanced thing I've ever worked on," Dr. Driscoll said.

At that moment Hank presented what he had ready for us.

A handheld time machine.

It was the size of a tablet with a black transparent screen. In the middle of it was a rotating Earth with a red outline around it. On the top of the screen was a white bar where I could pick the time period I wanted. On the bottom were icons that included medical supplies I would need, a notepad, video diary, list of animals I would encounter, and an "SOS" icon that would alert Dr. Driscoll if anything happened to us.

Dr. Driscoll and I met at a science convention, and he told me about a time machine he had been working on for the past few years. And I told him about my park idea.

Agreeing to help me, Dr. Driscoll built a couple of prototypes he used to send himself messages five minutes into the past. Then he was able to build a portal he used to travel one minute into the future.

As he was showing us how it worked, my hands were shaking with excitement.

I took a deep breath to ask, "Can we see it in action?"

"We certainly can," Dr. Driscoll said.

He tapped on the North America icon, and it enlarged on the screen. Then Dr. Driscoll dragged the latitude and longitude lines to the location of the Institute. When he tapped the "ACTIVATE" button, Ulysses and I watched with wide eyes as the lights began to flicker and the room began to shake. A small dot appeared in front of us! Then the dot expanded into the portal, and a long tunnel formed inside it.

We walked through the portal, where we saw our past selves, and we couldn't believe what was happening. When we walked back through the portal to the present to close it, we were still shaking.

"It works, all right," Ulysses said as we laughed.

"Hank, you've really outdone yourself with this time machine," I said.

"Thank you, Doug. Oh, before you go, my teammate Greg has something for you," Dr. Driscoll said as Greg walked in.

Greg Parker had helped design the wrist time machines. He also helped design the small portals they, too, could open.

He brought over a box full of what looked like watches.

Ulysses and I looked at them closely and realized they were wrist time machines.

Along with the time they also had some icons.

Dr. Driscoll and his team spent the day teaching us how to use the handheld and wrist time machines. They taught us what each icon did and spend a lot of time teaching us about the "SOS" icon. They even warned us what *not* to do.

After seeing how everything worked, Ulysses and I realized we needed someone to oversee the time machines, making sure we brought everything we needed on our expedition and especially making sure we brought everything back.

We took Dr. Driscoll aside and asked, "Hank, would you mind if we borrow Greg to join our team for this first expedition? We realized how technical the time machines are, so we figured Greg would be a big help to us."

"Of course, but you have to ask Greg."

"Hey, Greg, Ulysses and I were talking, and after seeing how well you helped design the time machines, would you like to join my team and help bring back dinosaurs to our park?" I asked.

"I would love to! Thank you so much for this opportunity, Doug," Greg said happily.

"Can you fly out tomorrow morning? I'll have someone pick you up at the airport to take you to the park."

"Yes," Greg said.

"Okay, great. I'll make the arrangements for you tonight. Hank, thank you again for all your help and the effort you put into these," I said.

"You're very welcome, Doug. Let me know how everything goes at the park, and if you need any help just call me."

"I certainly will." We shook hands.

After Ulysses and I left Dr. Driscoll's lab, we boarded the plane and headed back to the park, where I spent the night finishing the list.

The next day, with the list completed I went over to the control room, where I found Ulysses installing a motion sensor overlooking the holding pen. When I brought the animal back, the sensor would activate the large door on the holding pen and keep the animal in.

"Morning, Ulysses, how did you sleep?"

"I hardly slept at all. I was too excited. What about you?"

"I didn't sleep a wink. I spent the whole night thinking that we are actually going back in time, and we're going to see real-life dinosaurs!" I said. "Since we have everything up and running, why don't we go get the rest of our team—Jen, Lauren, and Kevin."

"Absolutely, let's do it," Ulysses said, and we headed off.

I chose Kevin Walton for my team because he's a survivalist. He knows how to live in the wilderness by finding clean water and food safe to eat. He also knows how to build a shelter to protect himself from the weather and build fire to keep warm.

Jen Davis is a field biologist who has traveled the world studying animal behavior. She's also helped preserve areas for endangered species.

Lauren Turner is my field veterinarian. She's spent her whole life taking care of animals. She's even checked the health of animals before they were transported to a safer location.

Deep in the Florida Everglades, Kevin and Jen were with their rookie teammate, Lauren, checking their trail cameras for an endangered female Florida panther they were tracking.

They walked down a small game trail amongst some large brush until Kevin spotted their next trail camera.

"Let's see if this one caught anything," he said.

"I hope so. The others didn't show anything," Jen said.

They took the memory card out of the camera and Jen placed it into her tablet.

"Let's see what we got," Lauren said.

They scanned through the pictures, but saw more common animals, mainly deer.

"Well, at least the deer are around here," Kevin said.

"But still nothing of the panther. She must be hiding in the thicker brush," Jen suggested.

They scrolled through the pictures until they spotted something on the last few photos.

When they zoomed in they were surprised to see it was the panther!

"Wow, look at her!" Lauren said happily.

Jen agreed. "I was hoping she was still here!"

"Wait a second, what's that next to her?" Kevin asked.

They swiped to the next photo and were amazed to see there were cubs with her!

"No way, she has cubs!" Jen said in shock.

"They look to be about three weeks old," Lauren said.

"That's going to be great for their population," Kevin said.

After they reset the trail camera, the team suddenly heard something breaking the quietness of the swamp. They looked up and saw a helicopter fly overhead.

"Who's that?" Lauren asked.

"That's Doug. He texted me they were coming to get us," Jen replied.

* * *

Kevin, Lauren, and Jen emerged from the swamp when my helicopter landed in the middle of a clearing. Ulysses and I got out and greeted Kevin's team with hugs, but I gave Jen the biggest hug.

"How are you guys?" Kevin asked.

"We're good and everything is set up at the park. We also picked up the time machine yesterday," Ulysses said.

"Really! Where is it? Can we see it?" they all asked in unison.

"You sure can. It's back at the park under lock and key," I said.

We all got into the helicopter to head back to the park.

Along the way Kevin asked, "Are we the only members of your team you invited, Doug?"

"No, I talked to Lois and Travis this morning. They're driving down to the park. I also invited one of Dr. Driscoll's assistants to join us, the one who helped build the time machine."

Lois Jackson is my lead tracker. She has traveled to some of the most remote areas to search for rare animals. With the help of the locals, she's managed to help find animal species not seen very often by humans.

Travis Grant is a field medic. He's very experienced in emergency medical situations. With his supplies he's prepared for nearly any type of injury.

We flew across the Everglades until we touched down near my office.

When we walked in we saw Greg talking with Lois, Travis, and the park keeper, Apollo Griswold.

Apollo is in charge of building the enclosures for the animals. He's done many jobs in zoos constructing enclosures for large predators.

"Glad you could make it, Greg. Guys, this is Greg. He'll be joining our team," I said.

"Nice to meet you, Greg," they all said.

"So, where is the time machine?" Kevin asked.

"It's right over here." I walked over to my wall safe. "Here it is." I presented them with the time machine, and they all looked at it in amazement.

"Here, we made these for you guys too." Greg showed them the wrist time machines.

"What are these, fancy watches, Greg?" Kevin asked as we laughed.

"No, these are wrist time machines. They have all the same features as the main time machine, along with their own portals."

"Cool, so in case of an emergency we can open our own portals?" Jen asked.

"Exactly. All right, guys, with everything in place, are we ready to head off on our first adventure?" I asked.

"Yes, we are!"

Chapter Two

We were all very excited as we loaded up our camping gear and food supplies before we headed down to the portal site.

On the way out Kevin asked, "Wait, before we go, can we see the list you've been talking about, Doug?"

"Oh, yes. Thank you for reminding me, Kevin."

I tapped on one of the icons on the time machine and showed my team the list. They all looked at it in surprise on how many animals we were going after.

"The first one we're going to find is a T. rex-like predatory dinosaur called the Abelisaurus," I said.

With anticipation, my team headed down to the portal site.

"Great timing on going for the Abelisaurus, Doug. My team just finished up the enclosure for it and we made sure it's exactly like when the Abelisaurus was alive," Apollo said.

"Perfect—that's why I hired you. You're great at what you do."

"Thank you, Doug. That means a lot."

After I shook hands with Apollo and Ulysses, they wished us luck on our first mission, and I placed the time machine in my satchel and headed down to meet with my team. To find the Abelisaurus, we had to go to Argentina in the Late Cretaceous period, eighty million years ago.

I saw everyone waiting for me, so I started to run because I was so excited.

"C'mon, Doug, let's see how the time machine works," Travis said.

"All right, all right, guys, hold your horses."

"Don't you mean dinosaurs, Doug?" Kevin asked.

"Um…no," I said as we all laughed.

I was holding the time machine and my hands were shaking so much, I was worried I wouldn't be able to move the lines to the correct coordinates.

I had to calm down, take my time, and breathe.

I tapped on Argentina and carefully moved the lines to the exact location we wanted to go to and set the time to eighty million years ago.

I looked up at my team and saw they were all looking at the time machine with wide eyes and big smiles.

"Well, guys, get ready to be the first humans to ever lay eyes on a living dinosaur. Are we ready?"

"Let's go already, push the button!" they all yelled.

I tapped the "ACTIVATE" button, and then our excitement was even more exaggerated as a small circle hovered right in front of our faces before expanding into the portal.

As our eyes adjusted to the light, we saw the portal was a long tunnel where we could see the past awaiting us. Around it was a purple glow. We could feel the powerful electrical currents moving through our bodies.

We looked at the portal in awe before Jen asked, "Hey, Doug, is it safe to go through this thing?"

"When you go through you will feel a little tingling, but don't worry, it won't hurt a bit. At least I don't think it will. You go first." I laughed.

"Very funny, Doug."

With our gear ready, we set off to Argentina in the Late Cretaceous, eighty million years ago.

We walked through the portal, getting closer and closer to the end. We were getting so close the excitement of seeing the past overwhelmed us! Then the muggy Florida air was soon replaced by a hot, arid climate.

We looked around. Argentina was an amazing place, with large valleys and barren ground covered in small shrubs. Groves of broad-leaf trees, called conifers, were spread throughout the area. Rocky hills surrounded us. A large mountain range was off in the distance. The sky was clear and blue.

I pressed the "DEACTIVATE" button on the time machine, and the portal expanded a few times before shrinking and disappearing.

We walked around until we found a large river snaking its way through the valley and decided to set up camp next to the river because in nature, prey and predator are attracted to water.

We set up camp underneath a grove of trees so we could observe any dinosaurs coming down to drink and stay out of sight of predators.

With the camp set up I gathered up my team and said, "Okay, guys, I know we've had to watch out for obvious dangers when tracking large predators, but this time we have to be on full alert. All we have is one partial skull of the Abelisaurus, so we don't know a lot about its behavior. But there are other dangers to be concerned about."

Back in Argentina between a hundred and sixty-six million

years ago, herds of long-necked dinosaurs called Sauropods traveled across the land. Hunting these giants were predatory animals called Abelisaurids, which were T. rex-like animals with big heads and powerful jaws.

With our mission about to begin, Jen suggested, "With plenty of vegetation in the valleys, the herbivores will be gathered there. Also, the hills here could provide excellent vantage points for any hungry predators."

"Okay then, Jen, you, Kevin, Greg, and I will head into the valley. Travis, you take Lauren and Lois with you into the hills. Guys, be safe and stay in contact with each other because we're in unchartered territory now," I said.

With the teams divided we headed off to find the Abelisaurus.

Chapter Three

While my team and I were walking through the valley, we were looking for signs of the Abelisaurus, such as tracks, piles of scat, or territorial marks on the trees.

We walked through a grove of trees and into a large clearing where the trees around us were so tightly packed together, it was hard to see behind them. The thickness of the trees would allow a large predator to easily stalk its prey.

When we got into the middle of the clearing, we realized something: There was not a single sound. No herbivores were bellowing in the distance, no predators were roaring, not even an insect.

We knew prey animals will go silent when they sense a predator is nearby.

So, we began to wonder what was keeping the animals silent.

Were we already in the heart of Abelisaurus territory? Was the Abelisaurus stalking us? Or maybe the herbivores sensed the Abelisaurus was nearby.

"I'm on edge right now with there being no sound," Jen said nervously.

"If the animals are being silent because of a predator, then it must be the Abelisaurus," I said.

"With all this open space the Abelisaurus could easily outrun us," Kevin said.

"There could also be more than one," Greg said.

"If the Abelisaurus does hunt in packs, we're in big trouble," Jen said.

We slowly made our way through the clearing until it opened into a large valley where we saw a herd of Sauropods.

We walked up to them and saw they were Overosaurus. Excited to come face-to-face with our first dinosaurs, we stood there in awe with our jaws wide open. Our hearts pounded faster and faster as the little kid in each of us wanted to come out and just touch the amazing animals that were standing in front of us.

The Overosaurus were twenty-eight feet long and weighed three tons. They had long necks with small heads. On their snouts were soft-tissue nasal structures. They were walking on four muscular legs. The males were covered in rough, light green scaly skin, and the females were covered in light brown scaly skin. On their backs were small armored plates, with small spikes on their flanks and front halves of their tails.

We noticed one large male who had red quills on the back of his head and the end of his tail. On his chin was a bright red wattle. We also saw he had several scars from past predator attacks.

We had seen a lot of impressive animals in our adventures, but nothing as outlandish as a herd of Sauropods.

"I can't believe we're actually looking at real dinosaurs!" Kevin said with a big smile on his face.

"These guys are even more impressive than I thought they were going to be," Jen said.

"I love how they have that armor and those spikes on their bodies," Greg said.

"I always wondered if Sauropods really did have quills," I said.

We saw that most of the adults were feeding on the trees. In the middle of the herd, the juveniles were feeding on the shrubs, with some of the adults forming a protective ring around them. The other adults were feeding on the shrubs by swaying their necks from side to side. Instead of chewing they were stripping the leaves off before swallowing them whole.

While the herd was feeding, the lead—or alpha male as they're called—was patrolling around the edge of the herd, keeping an eye out for predators.

When he approached us, my team and I moved out of his way so we didn't make him nervous.

"Up close you can really see how bright his quills and wattle are," Greg said.

"Having bright colors shows which males are more dominant," Jen said.

"In the past, he's done well with defending his herd," Kevin said.

"I wonder how many of those scars are from the Abelisaurus?" I said.

"Sauropods would be a perfect prey source for Abelisaurus, so good chance most of them are," Jen said.

When he walked past, the alpha stared down at us.

But then suddenly he turned his body and began to swing his tail! Then he began to pound the ground with his front legs!

My team and I backed up as the alpha continued to pound the ground. But then he reared up on his back legs before facing us and inflating his nasal sacs.

Behind him the herd huddled together while the juveniles gathered up behind them. We saw a couple of other younger males rearing up and swaying their tails.

Suddenly, we felt something standing right behind us!

We turned around to see a young male Aerosteon.

I quickly got my team up a nearby hill as the Aerosteon walked up to the alpha.

He lowered his body into a crouching position, and the alpha continued to swing his tail.

Instead, the Aerosteon began to make his way toward the herd.

He slowly walked through the herd, swaying his head from side to side, seeking a member of the herd that was old, injured, or sick.

Near the back of the herd, the Aerosteon spotted a juvenile trying to huddle with the adults. As he passed by him, the Aerosteon stared down the young Overosaurus before moving on.

With everything seemingly safe, the herd began to settle down. When the juvenile spotted a small shrub, he walked away from the herd to feed on it, all the while watching where the Aerosteon walked off to.

He began to feed on the shrub, but the Aerosteon came running up behind him and jumped onto his side and tried to scratch him with his large claws. The young Overosaurus quickly shook him off and started to run!

The Aerosteon chased after him, trying to grab his neck, but then the alpha came running up to help the juvenile. When he got the juvenile behind him, the alpha reared up and flared his front legs. Then the Aerosteon backed down.

Modern predators fail more often than they succeed since they always risk injury or death when hunting. Even dinosaurs will back down when they sense danger.

After the alpha made sure the juvenile was okay, he got him back in with the herd before leading them off into the valley.

While he watched them leave, the Aerosteon lay down on the ground.

The Aerosteon was sixteen feet long and weighed a thousand pounds. He had long arms with three-fingered hands, and twelve-inch claws on his first fingers. He was covered in rough, light blue scaly skin. On the back of his neck was a black line. He had an elongated snout full of serrated teeth. Above his eyes were two red triangular-shaped crests.

"That was a really awesome battle!" Greg said with excitement.

"It was cool to see the alpha male actually come in and defend the juvenile from the predator," Jen said.

"I'm impressed how the Aerosteon was relying more on his claws instead of his teeth to hunt the young Overosaurus," Kevin said.

"I was really hoping to see what a battle between a Sauropod and Theropod would have actually been like," I said happily.

After the herd left, the Aerosteon got up and walked off into the valley.

I tapped on the "PHONE" icon on my wrist time machine and called up Travis.

"Hey, Doug, how's your search going?" Travis asked when he answered.

"Good, we just ran into a young Aerosteon attacking an Overosaurus herd."

"You got to see two dinosaurs already!?" Lois asked in surprise.

"Yeah, we saw a whole herd of them," Kevin said.

"This is so cool. I can wait to see what else is around here!" Lauren said.

"Thank you for letting us know, Doug. We'll keep an eye out for him," Travis said.

"No problem, Travis. You guys stay safe."

"You too, Doug," Travis said, and I shut off the video.

With daylight fading, my team and I continued with our search.

Chapter Four

Meanwhile over in the hills, Travis and his team were searching for the Abelisaurus possibly stalking prey. They were also keeping an eye out for the Aerosteon.

"It's insane that Doug's team encountered an Aerosteon already instead of the Abelisaurus," Lauren said.

"Doug did say it was a young one, so he might be roaming for new territory," Lois said.

"If it's a young one, then that just makes you wonder where the adults could be," Travis said.

The team walked down a small hill over a rocky outcrop where a small lizard was basking in the sun before scurrying off.

At the base of the hill they walked into a clearing with clusters of trees around it.

They walked through the clearing until Lois noticed something different about the shrubs. She examined them closer before realizing they had been fed on. "Hey, guys, check this out. It looks like a group of herbivores has been here," she said.

"How fresh are these?" Lauren asked.

"Probably within the last ten minutes," Lois said.

They followed the sign behind a grove of trees, where they found a creche of juvenile Overosaurus.

They were seven feet long and weighed three hundred pounds. They had short snouts and big eyes. They didn't have armored plates on their backs or small spikes on their flanks. They were covered in rough, light brown scaly skin.

They stared at the creche in excitement as they slowly made their way toward them, trying not to scare them off.

"Wow, I wasn't expecting to see a group of juvenile Sauropods!" Lois said in excitement.

"Look how adorable they are too," Lauren said.

"I always thought the juveniles would be sticking close to the adults with predators like the Abelisaurus roaming around," Travis said.

While the juveniles were feeding, one of them walked over to a shrub. When she bent down to feed on the shrub, a head suddenly popped out of the ground.

When more of them appeared and came out of their burrow, Travis and his team saw they were Gasparinisaura.

The team watched in amazement as the flock scanned around with their big eyes before some of the females rushed over to the shrubs and brought some leaves over to their young in the burrow.

While the rest of the flock was feeding on the shrubs, the alpha male ran up onto a large rock and perched, looking for predators.

The Gasparinisaura were four feet long and weighed ten pounds. They had small bird-like heads with big eyes and tiny beaks. They were covered in smooth, light brown scaly skin, and the males had white stripes on their backs and tails. The juveniles had short snouts with big eyes. They were covered in soft, downy feathers.

"Right now, I'm trying to wrap my head around these dinosaurs in front of me that are living in burrows." Travis chuckled.

"That's just like Doug to hold off on the surprises that await us,"

Lois said as they laughed.

"At least we're learning new things as we go," Lauren said.

After one of the males left his burrow, the team decided to examine it to see what it was like. They walked up to the burrow and took their flashlights out to look inside.

The burrow went down about six feet on a small angle. The mouth of the burrow was about three feet wide. The burrows were full of dry leaves for bedding. There were also remnants of eggshells from when the juveniles hatched.

"These remind me of a hyena den," Lois said in surprise.

"The walls are well constructed too," Travis said.

"The Gasparinisaura must've really put in some time and energy into building these," Lauren said.

After they backed away from the burrow, Lois noticed one of the Overosaurus feeding on a shrub. Not wanting to miss the opportunity, the team carefully reached up and began to pet the young dinosaur. As they felt the roughness of her skin, they could only think, *Wow, we're actually touching a real dinosaur!* They petted her back and could feel the bits of armored plates just starting to appear.

But then the young Overosaurus lifted her head up and stared at Lois with big eyes and sniffed her before licking her face. Lauren and Travis couldn't help but laugh.

"How does it feel to be kissed by a dinosaur, Lois?" Travis asked.

"Gooey," Lois said in disgust.

Suddenly the alpha male Gasparinisaura stood up, and the rest of the flock lifted their heads and froze. Then they all quickly ran into their burrows as the young Aerosteon appeared.

The Aerosteon chased after the flock, narrowly missing one as it reached its burrow just in the nick of time.

The Aerosteon spotted the creche and ran after them!

The Aerosteon quickly caught up with the juvenile that licked Lois's face and slashed her side with his claw. As the juvenile began to slow down, the Aerosteon grabbed her neck and she collapsed to the ground!

Knowing the smell of the kill could attract other predators, the team quietly moved out of the area so they didn't get the Aerosteon's attention.

But then the loud sound of a tree limb snapping echoed from behind a nearby tree.

The Aerosteon looked over and noticed a large silhouette!

The team followed his gaze to a female Abelisaurus standing before the Aerosteon.

She slowly started to walk toward him, and the Aerosteon stood his ground.

She got closer and closer while the Aerosteon began to flush blood into his crests, turning them a bright red.

The Abelisaurus walked up to him, pushing him away from his kill, and then she began to display her throat pouch. When she made a bluff charge, the Aerosteon ran off.

When she reached down to feed on the carcass, the Aerosteon swiftly came running around her. Just as he was about to jump onto her, the Abelisaurus quickly swung her powerful tail and flung him through the air! The Aerosteon landed and skidded across the ground, sending dirt and rocks flying.

The Aerosteon struggled to get up while the Abelisaurus towered over him, but before she could bite him, the Aerosteon quickly escaped!

"I was expecting that to be an all-out fight," Travis said in shock.

"Normally predators avoid each other, and the only confrontations they get involved in are over kills," Lauren said.

"Now we know the Abelisaurus is an opportunistic animal, which is an animal that takes advantage of other predators' food," Lois said.

The Abelisaurus was twenty-three feet long and weighed two tons. She had a large head with a bumpy ridge on her snout and two round crests above her eyes. She had two short arms and walked on two muscular legs.

After the Abelisaurus fed on what was left on the carcass, she walked off into the hills.

Curious to see where she would go, the team decided to follow her to a couple of large hills covered in tall trees and blanketed in small shrubs. At the base of the hills was a large open valley. There were rub marks on some of the trees, marking the boundaries of her territory.

The Abelisaurus walked into a small section of trees in between the hills and lay down on the ground.

When it started to get late, I called up Travis and told them to meet us back at camp.

Back at base camp I asked, "What did you guys see in the hills?"

"Well, other than the seeing the Aerosteon, we found a female Abelisaurus!" Lois said happily.

"Really, what did she look like?" I asked with excitement.

"Along with looking like a T. rex, she was covered in rough, light green scaly skin. She had a gray ridge on her snout and round appendages above her eyes. Along her back were rows of brown bumps," Travis said as I sat down to catch my breath.

"How did she look?" Jen asked.

"She was in really good health. The Aerosteon attempted to attack her, but she was able to fend him off," Lauren said.

"Where did she go?" Greg asked.

"We followed her to a forested section overlooking a large valley," Lois said.

"Then that's where we're heading in the morning," I said.

When night fell we all turned in for the night.

Chapter Five

The next morning, Jen, Travis, and I headed over to the Abelisaurus territory. Kevin took Lauren, Lois, and Greg with him into the hills surrounding the valley to see if the Abelisaurus was patrolling around for food.

Along the way Travis asked, "What are we going to do when we find the Abelisaurus?"

"I want to see what her behavior is like. What we learn from her can give us a plan on how to get her back to the park," I said.

"We can even see what her hunting behavior is like," Jen said.

We walked through the hills until we found the valley. As we got closer to her territory, the air was as silent as it could be, but this time there was a good reason: No herbivore wants to be close to the territory of an animal that could eat it.

We walked behind some of the trees to avoid being spotted by the Abelisaurus in case she was still there, until we found a well-used path leading directly into the Abelisaurus territory.

"Looks like she's using the trees to provide cover while she comes in and out," I said.

"That would be a good way to stay out of sight from any rival Abelisaurus that wants to take over her territory," Jen said.

We were making our way down the path when an uneasy feeling of not being welcome came over us.

Then we were startled by what sounded like a large tree limb snapping!

We quickly looked around but saw nothing.

"I'm scared, Doug," Jen said nervously.

"Don't worry, I'm here." I tried to comfort her, but I was trying not to show I was scared myself.

When I had her territory in sight, I said to my team, "I can't see if she's there or not. What I want you guys to do is go to the top of that ridge and around to the back, and I'll go directly through where she comes in and out and see if I can find out where she went."

"You got it, Doug," Travis said.

"Be careful." Jen gave me a hug.

After the hug, I was in my own world, but soon snapped back into reality and headed into the territory of the Abelisaurus.

I walked farther and farther into the Abelisaurus' territory, looking for clues that would tell me where she might've gone.

I looked down and noticed a track in the dirt. It was the classic Theropod track. Like a bird, it had three toes with the biggest in the middle, and it showed the Abelisaurus was bipedal, meaning it walked on two legs, and not a quadruped, which is an animal that walks on four legs.

I looked at the direction the track was facing and saw it was heading to where my team was hiding!

I quickly took out my wrist time machine, but before I could tap the "PHONE" app, I suddenly felt a warm breath down my neck.

I slowly turned around to see a mouthful of serrated teeth, and when I looked up, I was face-to-face with the Aerosteon!

I attempted to run when I felt a powerful force hit my back that sent me flying forward a few feet, and I realized he hit me with the bony crests above his eyes! It took me a second to catch my breath. I blew the dirt off my face, and the rocks painfully rubbed against my chest. I tried to crawl away but the Aerosteon swung his small but powerful arm and slashed my leg with his big claw! He started to drag me away and I kicked his snout with my left foot, but he would not let go!

He dragged me back farther and farther, the claw sinking deeper and deeper in my leg. The pain was so unbearable I thought the claw was going to poke out the other side, but I needed to find a way to escape his grip!

Suddenly the Abelisaurus appeared, and not wanting to give me up, the Aerosteon flared his arms, and in doing so released me from his death grip. I realized I was free and about ten feet away from this hungry animal who wanted me for lunch. I looked around and spotted a large boulder I knew I could hide behind. As I attempted to stand, the pain hit me and I fell to the ground.

Desperate to get to safety, I crawled toward the boulder. Knowing I was still in danger, I looked back and saw the Abelisaurus chasing the Aerosteon out of her territory!

※ ※ ※

On the other side of the Abelisaurus territory, Jen and Travis were hiding behind a tree watching the whole thing. Jen was paralyzed with fear, but both she and Travis were frantically trying to think of a way to get the attention of the Abelisaurus, so they could help Doug out of the dangerous situation.

After the Abelisaurus drove the Aerosteon out of her territory, she turned and Jen could see her heading for Doug's hiding spot! She whispered to herself, "Doug, don't move! Don't move!" She didn't want to use her "PHONE" app because she knew it would get the attention of the Abelisaurus and might put Doug right back in danger.

I hid behind the boulder, trying not to move so the Abelisaurus wouldn't see me. I could see her silhouette walking in the opposite direction. I started to stand but the brim of my hat clipped the edge of the boulder and knocked over a few small rocks! The sound got the attention of the Abelisaurus, so she walked over in my direction to investigate.

I started to stand up, but then I saw her approaching, so I ducked down as the Abelisaurus appeared right over me! She lowered her head next to the boulder, and I could see the front of her snout.

She sniffed the air and I knew she could smell the blood from my wound.

She slowly turned her head in my direction, and a rock came

flying from the woods behind her! She whipped her head around to see what hit her. Then a second rock hit her, and she walked off to investigate.

Just then Jen and Travis came running up to me, and Jen gave me a big hug.

"Glad you're all right. But that was amazing to watch. You were very brave, but please don't scare me like that again," she said.

Knowing the Abelisaurus could return at any time, Travis helped me to my feet and carried me behind some trees and out of sight.

Travis looked at my leg and said, "This looks a lot worse than it is."

"What do you mean?" I asked.

"The scratch is pretty deep, so you could be at risk of getting an infection. I'll stitch you up, but we'll have to look at it when we get back to the park."

Travis took some medical thread from his bag to stitch up my leg and close the wound. Then he wrapped my leg to protect it from the elements.

As Travis finished up, I said, "Thanks for getting her attention with those rocks."

"No problem. It looked like you could use some help." Travis laughed.

"Gee, you think? Did you guys see where she was heading?" I asked.

"Yeah, she was heading for the valley over the hill," Jen said.

Travis helped me up and we went off to find the Abelisaurus. We caught up with her while she walked amongst the hills.

We followed close behind at a safe distance until she suddenly stopped and sniffed the air. Then she began to slowly walk behind a grove of trees like she was stalking something.

She walked to the edge of the tree line, where she spotted a herd of Overosaurus feeding on the trees. Near the back of the herd, there was an old male that was having trouble keeping pace with the herd.

The Abelisaurus hid behind the trees, with the shadows providing camouflage for her. She zigzagged behind the trees, getting closer and closer to the old Overosaurus. Then she got behind a large tree and crouched. Her foot claws tightly gripped the ground.

Before the old Overosaurus could react, the Abelisaurus quickly ran up to him and bit his shoulder. As she clamped down harder, the old Overosaurus shoved her and she lost her grip. He struggled to shift all his weight onto his three legs, and began to swing his tail. The Abelisaurus went in for a second attack, but the Overosaurus quickly hit her in the head with his tail. The Abelisaurus backed down.

As the old Overosaurus made his way back to the herd, we saw his wound was severe and he was already bleeding heavily.

"I can't believe that old Overosaurus managed to fend her off," Travis said in surprise.

"A lot of old animals can still have the strength to fend off attacks from predators," Jen said.

"Since he's already weak and now that he's injured, she will wait until he weakens even more before going in for the final attack," I said.

Modern predators, including lion prides and wolf packs, have been known to track injured prey after attacking them later when they were weak.

"I'm amazed how she relies on her head to attack prey," Travis said.

"Without any arms, her head and teeth are her main source of hunting," I said.

"With a short snout and serrated teeth, she's able to grasp and hold onto any struggling prey," Jen said.

Like the Tyrannosaurs, the Abelisaurids evolved bigger heads with powerful jaws and neck muscles for attacking prey. In doing so they reduced the size of their arms so they could remain balanced on their legs.

"With those short legs, I can see she doesn't rely on speed to chase down her prey," Jen said.

"Exactly—instead she relies on ambush," I said.

After the herd left, the Abelisaurus walked down a nearby hill to a small stream where she took a few sips.

Then she walked back to her territory and lay down to rest.

Chapter Six

Across from my team in the valley behind the Abelisaurus territory, Kevin's team was looking for the Abelisaurus when they heard
the commotion from the Abelisaurus attacking the old Overosaurus,
but the noise soon dissipated.

"What do you guys think Doug has planned to rescue the
Abelisaurus?" Lauren asked.

"Not sure, but I hope it's a safe plan," Greg said.

"Knowing Doug, it's probably not a safe plan," Kevin said as they
laughed.

"Yeah, probably not," Lois said.

As they were walking through the valley, Kevin's team came
across another herd of Overosaurus feeding on the shrubs. With
them was another flock of Gasparinisaura, running amongst the legs
of the Overosaurus and feeding on the shrubs.

The team watching the herd noticed the alpha male standing
guard next to one of the juveniles. When they got a clear look, Greg
noticed it had some injuries on its side, and that's when Greg recog-
nized the juvenile.

"Hey, Kevin, check it out—it's the juvenile the Aerosteon attacked!"

"Yeah, you're right, Greg."

Lauren finally got a clear look at the young animal and examined his injuries. She saw they were starting to heal up but were still serious.

"The Aerosteon left some bad scratches on him. So, it's a good thing the alpha is sticking by his side," Lauren said.

While the juvenile was feeding on a shrub, the alpha noticed another one of the juveniles starting to stray from the herd. He went over to get her back into the herd, but the injured juvenile was wandering away.

Then suddenly the Gasparinisaura flock ran in a panic as the Aerosteon ran up to the injured juvenile and scratched his side! The alpha attempted to rush to the juvenile's aid but the Aerosteon continued his attack. Then the Aerosteon jumped onto the side of the juvenile and knocked him to the ground!

But before the Aerosteon could grab the juvenile's neck, the alpha quickly came charging up to the Aerosteon and bolted into his side.

The Aerosteon hit the ground and skidded across it, leaving a deep impression in the dirt. He came to the edge of a large hill and nearly toppled down it but managed to catch himself with the claws on his feet.

The Aerosteon hunkered down as the alpha helped the juvenile back to his feet. After he got him back into the herd, the alpha led the herd away. The Aerosteon walked down the hill and into the valley.

"That has got to be the luckiest juvenile, having the alpha look after him," Lauren said.

"In elephant herds it's always the matriarch's job to watch over her herd," Kevin said.

"Looks like even dinosaurs were doing the same thing," Greg said.

"Makes you wonder what other secrets they're hiding," Lois said.

Kevin's team decided to continue their search. When it started to get late, they headed back to camp.

※ ※ ※

Back at camp while they were waiting, Kevin's team saw us coming, and they noticed Travis helping me walk.

"What happened to you, Doug?" Kevin asked.

"I was off making a new friend," I said.

"With who?" Lois asked.

"The Aerosteon," I said.

"Earlier we saw the alpha Overosaurus finally scare him off from the injured juvenile," Greg said.

Travis sat me down next to our campfire before taking off my bandages to look at my leg.

"Aw, that looks really bad," Lauren said with concern.

"Yeah, I'll rebandage it and we'll see how it does overnight," Travis said.

While Travis bandaged up my leg, Lois asked, "Did you guys

find the Abelisaurus?"

"We found her, but along with the Aerosteon, she almost made a meal of Doug," Jen said.

"I had it handled, Jen."

"While you were handling it, Doug, did you come up with a plan to rescue her?" Kevin asked.

"Yeah, we followed her to an open valley where she attacked an old Overosaurus. So, I figured if she finds food, then I'll run up to her and after I get her to chase me, I'll open the portal and lead her back to the park. You guys make sure she goes through before you follow us," I said.

"Why can't we just open the portal in front of her while she's walking through the valley so you don't have to put any stress on your leg?" Lois asked.

"Where'd be the fun in that?" I asked as we laughed.

After Travis bandaged up my leg, and with our plan set, my team and I turned in to rest up for our final day.

Chapter Seven

The next day I got up to check on my leg. It wasn't bleeding, but still looked bad.

When Jen woke up she asked, "Did you get any sleep with your leg like that?"

"Yeah, I got a few hours' sleep. It doesn't hurt as much as it did last night."

After Travis woke up, he checked on my leg, telling me, "It's looking good. How does it feel when you put pressure on it?"

"It hurts a little, but nothing I can't handle," I said.

Once the rest of my team woke up, we gathered up our camp and went to find the Abelisaurus.

We arrived at the Abelisaurus territory to pick up her trail. We walked through her territory until we found the path the Abelisaurus took to stalk the Overosaurus herd.

Along the way, with Lois in the lead, she looked down and noticed something in the dirt. "Hey, guys, here's a track!"

"Wow, it looks like a giant bird," Jen said in surprise.

"It's fresh too, probably within the last ten minutes, so she's close," Lois said.

We continued along until we found the valley where the Abelisaurus attacked the old Overosaurus.

Just then the Abelisaurus appeared out of the tree line across from us and walked up to the spot where she attacked the Overosaurus. She spotted a few drops of blood on the ground and sniffed them. Then she sniffed the air and began to walk into the valley to track the herd.

We followed close behind her for over an hour as she continued through the valley, stopping to sniff the ground a couple more times.

Just a little further on, the Abelisaurus walked to the top of a hill, and below her in a large valley was the herd. Near the back of the herd was the old male she'd attacked.

We could see he was struggling to keep up with his herd. Every time he put pressure on his leg, it would wobble. We knew soon he would collapse and the herd would leave him behind.

The Abelisaurus snuck up behind a small grove of trees to wait. With his injuries and the heat, the old Overosaurus stopped while the herd continued. Then, finally succumbing to his injuries, he collapsed to the ground!

The Abelisaurus walked up to him, but when the Overosaurus lifted his tail a bit, she sensed he could still pose a danger, so she decided to wait just a little longer.

Not too long into waiting, the old Overosaurus laid his head on the ground and died from his injuries. The Abelisaurus looked around to make sure the Aerosteon wasn't anywhere around. Then she began to eat.

"Man, look at how she eats," I said in amazement.

"She's actually eating like a bird of prey. Using her powerful leg to hold her food down while she uses her teeth," Jen said.

I said to my team, "Okay, guys, I'm going to get the portal set. When she chases me through it, stay a safe distance behind her before you follow us, and then go through the door on the left side of the fence."

"Good luck, Doug. Be safe," they said.

I took the time machine out of my satchel and typed in the co-ordinates back to the park. I tapped the "ACTIVATE" button and the portal opened.

I ran up to the Abelisaurus, and when she saw me, she started to chase me to protect her kill. I led her through the portal and back to the park.

I led her through a pathway that was fenced on both sides and to a large holding pen.

I scrambled through the pathway, and the motion sensor in the control room activated the gate door on the holding pen.

The Abelisaurus was breathing down my neck. I hurried as fast as I could to reach the door before it closed!

I ran past the door on the holding pen, taking a sharp right turn through an emergency door, before closing it as the Abelisaurus was trying to reach for me!

"Now that was fun!" I said to myself.

After I closed the door, I was happy I'd rescued the first dinosaur and the first animal for the park!

I was also relieved I managed to escape with my life.

Once the Abelisaurus was secured in the holding pen, I ran through another exit door over to the portal to see my team coming through.

Ulysses notified everyone in the park we had returned with the first dinosaur. While they all headed over to the observation deck to see her, Apollo drove up with my head vet, Olivia Gibbs.

Olivia oversaw taking care of all the animals in the park, making sure they were happy and healthy. She had spent her life volunteering at several zoos, helping with taking care of sick and young animals.

Olivia looked at the Abelisaurus, speechless, for a good few minutes before she finally spoke. "Wow, I can't believe I'm looking at a real dinosaur! She's amazing!"

She observed the Abelisaurus for a half hour, checking for any injuries or anything else that might've been harmful to the Abelisaurus.

"How is she, Olivia?" I asked.

"She looks in perfect health. I don't see any injuries on her. I saw she was eating well when Apollo and Ulysses gave her that large piece of meat. So, I think she's ready for her enclosure," Olivia said.

After I made sure the Abelisaurus was in good health, I met up with Travis in his office to have another look at my leg.

"The wound is starting to heal really well now, so I'll just bandage it up. In the meantime, what a story you'll have to tell about this someday," Travis said.

"How many people can say they got scars from a dinosaur?" I said.

"I know, right?" Travis said as we laughed.

Later that day Apollo's teammates backed up a Raptor pickup truck with a trailer to a large door on the other end of the holding pen.

They opened the door on the trailer, revealing a piece of meat in the front. Following the scent of the meat, the Abelisaurus loaded herself onto the trailer. Then she was brought over to her new home.

I was very happy with the enclosure. It had a wide-open area so the Abelisaurus could roam around. The ground was barren since grass didn't evolve in the time of the dinosaurs. There was a large grove of trees so she could get out of the sun when it got hot out and where she could sleep.

"Apollo, you and your team did a great job with the enclosure. I have no doubt she will love it here," I said.

"Thank you, Doug."

After the Abelisaurus was unloaded, she wandered around her enclosure until she lay down in the shade of the trees.

"Well, guys, while she settles in, let's go to the cafeteria to get something to eat," I said.

When we got to the cafeteria, we all sat down to enjoy our first victory meal. We were all still in shock that we were able to bring back the first dinosaur into the present.

"So, Doug, you never told us the name of your park," Kevin said.

"I'm not sure what to call it," I said.

"Well, since you did have a large list, and all those animals need their own territories, how about Prehistoric Territories," Jen suggested.

"You know, I like it! Prehistoric Territories it will be," I said happily.

"Are you happy with how successful our first mission was?" Greg asked.

"Yes, I am. This has been my dream my whole life," I said.

"Well then, are you ready for your next mission, Doug? I mean Dino Doug?" Ulysses asked.

"Dino Doug? Where did that come from?" Lauren laughed.

"I've known Doug for years and he always told me facts about prehistoric animals. So, one day I called him Dino Doug," Ulysses said.

"Sounds like a good name for him," Jen said.

"Guys, are we ready for our next mission?" I asked.

"We are ready!"

"Then I am ready for our next mission too."

With the park's first animal now living at the park, my team and I can get ready for our missions through time to rescue prehistoric animals and make them feel welcome right here at Prehistoric Territories.

Paleofacts
Abelisaurus
(ah-bell-eh-sore-us)

Meaning: Abel's Reptile, named in honor of paleontologist Roberto Abel, who found the dinosaur. This animal is known only from a partial skull measuring twenty-three inches long, lacking the lower jaw. With short arms this dinosaur couldn't grasp, so instead it relied on its powerful jaws to attack its prey.

Aerosteon
(air-oh-stee-on)

Meaning: Air Bone. Known from a partial skeleton, this animal got its name because of how hollow its bones were. Its wishbone also shows it had an air sac system like a bird to help it stay very active. The large claws on its first fingers were used to wound its prey.

Overosaurus
(oh-ver-oh-sore-us)

Meaning: Overo Reptile, named after the area where the fossils were found. Known from a partial skeleton, this medium-sized Sauropod relied on its tail and the armor covering its body to defend itself from the large predators in its habitat.

Gasparinisaura
(gas-pa-ree-nee-sore-ah)

Meaning: Gasparini's Reptile, named in honor of paleontologist Zulma Brandoni de Gasparini. This small bird-like dinosaur is known from several well-preserved skeletons. Recent fossil findings of its close relatives show that they lived in burrows to protect their young, so it's certainly possible Gasparinisaura did the same.

Size Chart

The size of an average man and the Abelisaurus, Aerosteon, Gasparinisaura, and Overosaurus.

Bibliography

The Princeton Field Guide to Dinosaurs, Paul, G.S. 2010 pg. 79.

www.geol.umd.edu/tholtz/dinoappendix.

Index

Glossary

Abelisaurids: A group of meat-eating dinosaurs found mainly in the southern part of the world.

Bipedal: An animal that walks on two legs.

Burrow: A hole dug into the ground by an animal.

Camouflage: How an animal conceals itself in its surroundings.

Creche: A nursery of baby animals.

Crest: A ridge structure on an animal's skull.

Display: To show off to one another.

Endangered: An animal on the verge of going extinct.

Evolve: To develop over time.

Flank: The side of an animal between the hips and ribs.

Flock: A group of animals that stick together.

Grasp: To hold firmly on something.

Habitat: The natural environment of an organism.

Herd: Several animals kept together.

Juvenile: A young animal.

Lack: Something that's missing.

Opportunist: Taking an opportunity despite the principles.

Outlandish: Having a foreign appearance.

Paleontologist: The science of ancient life on Earth.

Physicist: The science of the physics of the universe.

Predator: An animal that hunts other animals.

Prey: An animal hunted for food.

Quadruped: An animal that walks on four legs.

Sauropod: A group of long-necked dinosaurs.

Sub-Adult: A near mature animal.

Territory: The land belonging to one or more animals.

Track: Evidence that something has passed by.

Tyrannosaurs: A group of powerful predators with massive heads and strong jaws.

Unchartered: Without regulations.

Wishbone: A forked bone in the chest cavity of a bird.

About the Author

Kyle is a quiet yet intelligent, self-taught individual who's been fascinated with dinosaurs and prehistoric life for over twenty years. He has informed and captivated family and friends with an abundance of prehistoric facts and theories, including pronouncing the names of prehistoric animals, and sharing when they lived and how they survived in their habitat. Kyle enjoys his time volunteering as a Fossil Explainer at the American Museum of Natural History in New York City.

Prehistoric
Territories
Episode Two

After the adventure of searching for the Abelisaurus, Dino Doug and his team will now enter the world of the rhino. Amongst the ancient Miocene scrublands of Spain, they'll encounter animals very similar to the modern animals of the Serengeti. Lurking amongst the shadows will be predators unlike anything alive today.

CPSIA information can be obtained
at www.ICGtesting.com
Printed in the USA
BVHW052251300619
552333BV00005B/25/P

9 781478 751724